Mountain National Park

Like Orion, Stephanie Lowman enjoys traveling to new and exciting places, whether in real life or her imagination. She currently lives in Arvada, Colorado with her children, Osiris the Dog and Cassidy the Cat. She is also the illustrator of the books "Dreaming of Colorado" and "Dreaming of Arches National Park."

Grant Collier has been working as a photographer and writer since 1996 and is the author of 14 books. In producing this book, Grant used Photoshop to combine his photographs with the illustrations of animals drawn by Stephanie. You can view his other books at collierpublishing.com and his photography at gcollier.com.

Dreaming of Rocky Mountain National Park

Collier Publishing LLC

Arvada, CO

ISBN # 978-1-935694-42-7
Printed in South Korea

Published by Collier Publishing LLC
https://www.collierpublishing.com

Orion the Owl did not want to go to sleep.
He wanted to play with the bighorn sheep.

But his mom said
he must go to bed,

So he grudgingly
lay down his head.

He tossed and turned but drifted off at last,
And soon was dreaming of the distant past.

In his dream, an ancient world appeared.
It was magical, mysterious, and a little weird.

Inside, there were charming
birds flying across the land,

And old mossy trees that
were equally as grand.

But more impressive still was the mighty Triceratops.
It jolted the land as it walked, shaking the highest of treetops.

Also in the thicket was an armored dinosaur.
When danger was at hand, it hid on the forest floor.

Nearby, there were raptors at a lovely waterfall.
Orion thought these creatures were the strangest of them all.

Of course, no visit to
this bygone land would
ever be complete,

Without a sighting of
T. Rex escaping from
the midday heat.

Deeper in the forest, an icy world appeared.
It was wintry, wild, and not for the unprepared.

Orion flew into this new land, as only would the brave,
And met a woolly mammoth inside a vast ice cave.

Then he saw a giant sloth and two enormous short-faced bears,

None of which had walked this land in over 10,000 years.

Next to these massive beasts, Orion felt so small.
He was tired, anxious, and lonely most of all.

But then he discovered
another glowing sphere,

That might take him back
to the present year.

Within the lush forest, he found many of his friends,
Including a beaver, a marmot, and a little wren.

But the only humans here were like none he'd seen before.
They were Ute Indians, who lived in the days of yore.

They had no loud cars or distracting phones.
You could hear the bubbling brook instead of bad ringtones.

They spent their nights inside teepees or grass huts,
And made pottery and baskets to carry berries, seeds, and nuts.

They created spears and arrows out of nearby rocks,

And counted the days using stars instead of clocks.

They met each year to do the great Bear Dance.
There was singing, music, and hypnotic chants.

Orion was glad to no longer feel alone,
But he still wanted to get back home.

So he found a new
enchanted ball,

That led to a land
with fresh snowfall.

Orion's heart sank when he saw no one around,
But then he spotted a man far below on the ground.

The man was named Enos Mills,
And he loved hiking in the great white hills.

Enos dreamed of making this land a park,
That all could enjoy, whether human, elk, or lark.

Mr. Mills was an average, ordinary man,
But he convinced the president to approve his plan.

In this land where dinosaurs
and mammoths once roamed,

A national park would be
formed that to all could be home.

Orion asked Mr. Mills how to get back to his nest,
And the man pointed towards a small path to the west.

The path wound through the trees towards a bright light,
That now had become a most comforting sight.

All he had seen was more
than his mind could absorb,

As Orion soared through
one last dazzling orb.

But rather than finding an exotic new place,
He opened his eyes to his mom's loving embrace.

He told his mom about the places he'd seen,
And the wondrous animals he'd met in his dream.

Orion now knew the value of sleep.
It's an everyday gift that the wisest will reap.

As the sky filled with color and the moon said goodbye,
Orion flew higher and higher into the sky.

He was eager to find new places to see,
In this land of great peaks where all can live free.

Did you know?

- 68 million years ago, dense rainforests and swamps covered the land around Rocky Mountain National Park, and there was a shallow sea to the east.
- Mountains began to rise that would become the Rocky Mountains we know today.
- During this time, dinosaurs roamed across Colorado, including the Triceratops, the Tyrannosaurus Rex, the armored Edmontonia, and the Dromaeosaurids (who are often called raptors).
- Dinosaurs became extinct about 65 million years ago, after a giant asteroid struck the planet.

- Beginning around 2.7 million years ago, a series of ice ages covered Colorado's mountains with large glaciers.
- These glaciers carved out steep valleys and basins in present-day Rocky Mountain National Park.
- During this time, enormous mammals, including ground sloths, short-faced bears, and mammoths, roamed throughout the state.
- Most of these animals became extinct around 10,000 years ago, likely because of over-hunting and a changing climate.

- The first Native Americans entered Rocky Mountain National Park around 10,000 to 15,000 years ago, at the end of the last ice age.
- Beginning about 1,500 years ago, Native Americans began crafting the bow and arrow and making pottery. Many arrow points and pottery shards have been found in the park.
- Over the past 1,000 years, the main tribes that inhabited the park were the Ute, Shoshoni, and Arapaho.
- Due to cold winters at high altitudes, they mostly traveled through the park in the warmer months and did not live there year-round.

- Enos A. Mills was born in Kansas and moved to Colorado in 1884, at the age of 14.
- Enos made his first ascent of Longs Peak in 1885. He would later climb this mountain 296 more times!
- In the early 1900s, Enos began advocating in his writing and speeches for the creation of a national park around Longs Peak.
- On January 26, 1915, President Woodrow Wilson signed a bill establishing Rocky Mountain National Park as the 10th national park in the United States.
- Although the park was smaller than the one Enos envisioned, it has helped protect and preserve a very large area of the Rocky Mountains for over 100 years.

Dreaming of Rocky